362.29 A   Aretha, David.

Cocaine and crack

HOMESTEAD HS MEDIA CENTER
585394

DATE DUE			

DRUGS

COCAINE AND CRACK

A MyReportLinks.com Book

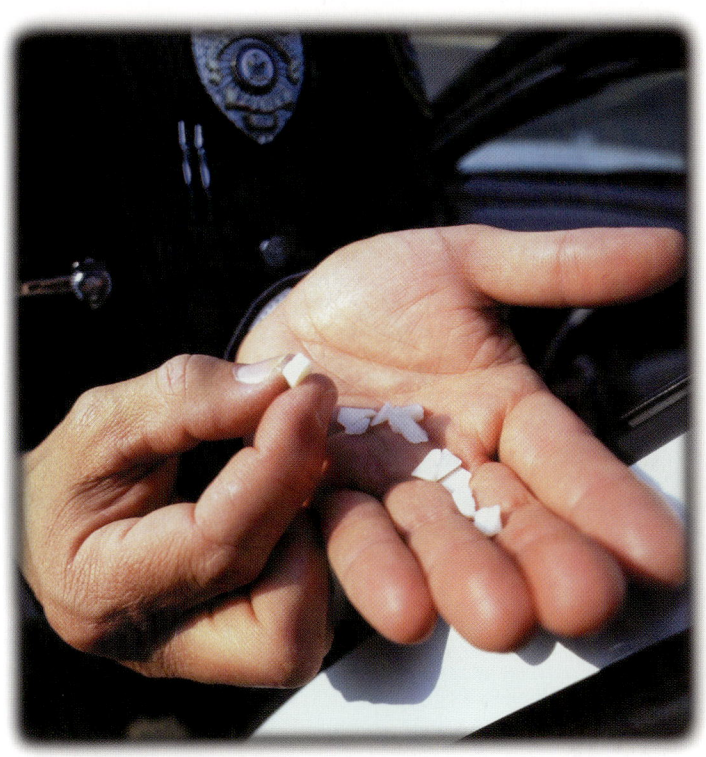

David Aretha

MyReportLinks.com Books
an imprint of

Enslow Publishers, Inc.
Box 398, 40 Industrial Road
Berkeley Heights, NJ 07922
USA

MyReportLinks.com Books

MyReportLinks.com Books, an imprint of Enslow Publishers, Inc. MyReportLinks® is a registered trademark of Enslow Publishers, Inc.

Copyright © 2005 by Enslow Publishers, Inc.

All rights reserved.

No part of this book may be reproduced by any means without the written permission of the publisher.

Library of Congress Cataloging-in-Publication Data

Aretha, David.
  Cocaine and crack / David Aretha.
    p. cm. — (Drugs)
  Includes bibliographical references and index.
  ISBN 0-7660-5276-1
  1. Cocaine—Juvenile literature. 2. Crack (Drug)—Juvenile literature. I. Title. II. Drugs (Berkeley Heights, N.J.)
  RC568.C6A74 2005
  362.29'8—dc22
                              2004007006

Printed in the United States of America

10 9 8 7 6 5 4 3 2 1

To Our Readers:
Through the purchase of this book, you and your library gain access to the Report Links that specifically back up this book.
The Publisher will provide access to the Report Links that back up this book and will keep these Report Links up to date on www.myreportlinks.com for five years from the book's first publication date.
We have done our best to make sure all Internet addresses in this book were active and appropriate when we went to press. However, the author and the Publisher have no control over, and assume no liability for, the material available on those Internet sites or on other Web sites they may link to.
The usage of the MyReportLinks.com Books Web site is subject to the terms and conditions stated on the Usage Policy Statement on **www.myreportlinks.com**.
A password may be required to access the Report Links that back up this book. The password is found on the bottom of page 4 of this book.
Any comments or suggestions can be sent by e-mail to comments@myreportlinks.com or to the address on the back cover.

Photo Credits: AP/Wide World Photos, pp. 11, 13; Clipart.com, p. 23; Digital Stock Photos: Government and Social Issues, pp. 1, 9, 20, 28, 40; Monitoring the Future Study, p. 36; MyReportLinks.com Books, p. 4; Narcotics Anonymous, p. 38; National Archives, pp. 17, 21, 30; National Court Reporters Association (NCRA), p. 42; National Drug Intelligence Center, pp. 18, 32; National Institute on Drug Abuse, pp. 14, 26; National Survey on Drug Use and Health, p. 22; Neuroscience for Kids, p. 25; Office of National Drug Control Policy, pp. 31, 35; Photos.com, p. 33; U.S. Drug Enforcement Administration, pp. 3, 43.

Cover Photo: Digital Stock Photos: Government and Social Issues (policeman); Photos.com (razor and cocaine).

Disclaimer: While the stories of abuse in this book are real, many of the names have been changed.

	Report Links	**4**
	Cocaine and Crack Facts	**9**
1	**Stories of Cocaine and Crack Abuse**	**10**
2	**History of Cocaine and Crack**	**16**
3	**Effects of Cocaine and Crack**	**23**
4	**Producing and Selling Cocaine and Crack**	**30**
5	**Avoiding Drugs and Getting Help**	**35**
	Glossary	**44**
	Chapter Notes	**45**
	Further Reading	**47**
	Index	**48**

About MyReportLinks.com Books

MyReportLinks.com Books
Great Books, Great Links, Great for Research!

The Internet sites listed on the next four pages can save you hours of research time. These Internet sites—we call them "Report Links"—are constantly changing, but we keep them up to date on our Web site.

Give it a try! Type http://www.myreportlinks.com into your browser, click on the series title, then the book title, and scroll down to the Report Links listed for this book.

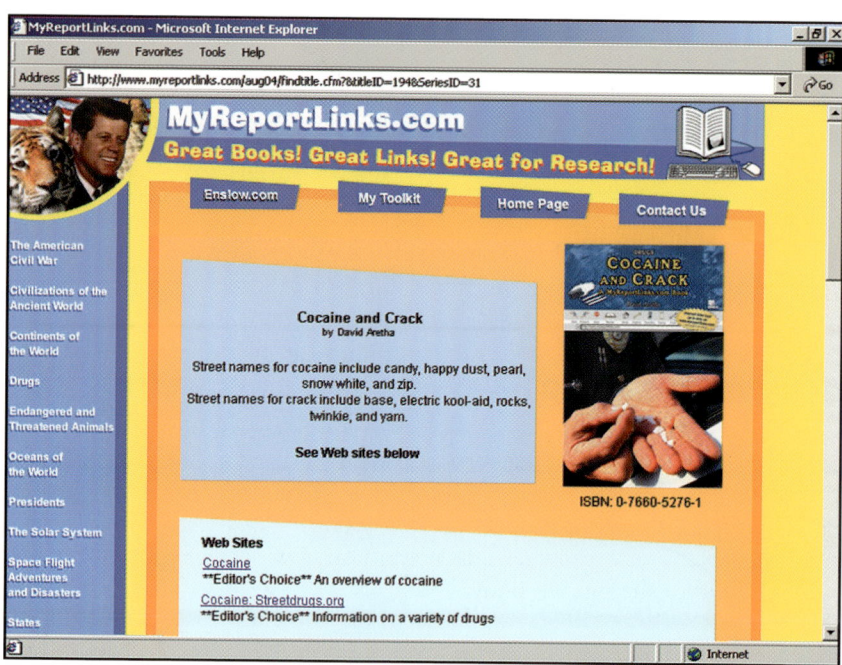

The Report Links will bring you to great source documents, photographs, and illustrations. MyReportLinks.com Books save you time, feature Report Links that are kept up to date, and make report writing easier than ever!

Please see "To Our Readers" on the copyright page for important information about this book, the MyReportLinks.com Web site, and the Report Links that back up this book.

Please enter **DRC1963** if asked for a password.

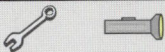   MyReportLinks.com Books

Tools Search Notes Discuss   Go!

Report Links

 The Internet sites described below can be accessed at
http://www.myreportlinks.com

Editor's choice

▶**Cocaine**
Information is provided on cocaine abuse, including health effects, treatment, legal consequences, production, and trafficking. Links to other resources, including government reports, are also provided.

Editor's choice

▶**Cocaine: Streetdrugs.org**
An overview of cocaine and crack is presented along with information on their effects, trafficking, and street names. Statistics on HIV/AIDS infection and crack addiction, as well as color pictures of cocaine, crack, and the coca plant are also included.

Editor's choice

▶**From Coca-Cola to Crack: A History of Cocaine in the United States**
Learn how cocaine was first introduced into the United States. Information is also provided on its early uses and the first signs of problems associated with addiction. The introduction of crack cocaine and its effects on society are discussed.

Editor's choice

▶**What You Need to Know About Drugs: Cocaine and Crack**
Developed for young people, this fact sheet explains what cocaine is and what it looks like. It also provides information on how cocaine is used and what it does to the human body.

Editor's choice

▶**Research Report Series: Cocaine Abuse and Addiction**
Read about cocaine use in the United States, including how it is used, its effects, effective treatments for abusers, and more.

Editor's choice

▶**NIDA for Teens: The Science Behind Drug Abuse**
Created with the help of teenagers, facts are provided on what drugs do to the body and brain. Games, quizzes, and animated illustrations teach concepts and relay information.

Any comments? Contact us: comments@myreportlinks.com   5

Back | **Forward** | **Stop** | **Review** | **Home** | **Explore** | **Favorites** | **History**

Report Links

The Internet sites described below can be accessed at
http://www.myreportlinks.com

▶ Coca Fact Paper: A Primer
Cocaine is derived from the coca plant. You will find data on plant varieties, history, growing, harvesting, and how the plant is processed into cocaine. Information on countries growing the crops is also included.

▶ Cocaine
Read about how cocaine affects the brain and nervous system. A brief history of cocaine is also included.

▶ Cocaine Abuse
Learn about cocaine and its long-term effects. Signs of abuse, risks to others, and treatment possibilities are also discussed.

▶ Cocaine and Crack
You will find detailed information on cocaine and crack cocaine in the government paper found on this Web site. Data is provided on the drugs' availability, demand, production, transportation, distribution, primary market areas, and future projections of how many people will abuse the drugs.

▶ Cocaine Anonymous
Read about the Twelve Steps of Recovery program, and find information on meetings, conventions, and literature for those interested in recovering from cocaine addiction. A section telling you how to find meetings in your area and a self-test for cocaine addiction are also included.

▶ Cocaine Use During Pregnancy
This Web site looks at the effects of taking cocaine while pregnant, and discusses the long-term outlook for children who are exposed to cocaine before birth.

▶ CocaineAddiction.com
The Narconon Arrowhead drug and alcohol rehabilitation program is described here. Learn the causes of addiction, cocaine facts, and research results. You will also find downloadable videos and information packs, free online assessments, and an "ask a question" form.

▶ Crack and Cocaine
Learn about the health hazards of using crack and cocaine, as well as the added danger of mixing them with alcohol. A statistical chart displaying cocaine use by students is also provided.

Any comments? Contact us: **comments@myreportlinks.com**

Report Links

The Internet sites described below can be accessed at http://www.myreportlinks.com

▶Drug-Free Communities Support Program
Discover a program that aims to help community groups reduce substance abuse among youths while creating drug-free environments.

▶Focus Adolescent Services
This site provides informative resources for teens on substance abuse, therapy, mental heath, emotional healing, anger management, behavioral problems, and more. A section on cocaine contains details on its use, effects, and treatment.

▶High School and Youth Trends
Information is provided on the use trends of specific drugs, such as cocaine. Data on how young people perceive the risk of harm, disapproval from friends, and the availability of the drug is given as well.

▶NAADAC, The Association for Addiction Professionals
NAADAC looks to create healthier families and communities through drug prevention, intervention, and quality treatment. It supports research and advocates policies and funding support for the prevention, understanding, and treatment of addictions.

▶Narcotics Anonymous
Based on the Twelve Steps, Narcotics Anonymous can be found in over one hundred countries. You can follow the links to find worldwide contact and meeting information. Bulletins, reports, and periodicals are also available for the reader.

▶National Council on Alcoholism and Drug Dependence, Inc.
This site contains lots of information written for youths, including a self-test that teenagers can take on how alcohol and drugs are affecting their lives. Educational materials, including pamphlets, posters, and videos, are available.

▶National Institute on Drug Abuse (NIDA)
Scientific information on drugs in the form of reports, papers, notes, news releases, and charts can be accessed at this site. You will learn about drug abuse, prevention, addiction, and treatment.

▶Not My Kid
The Not My Kid Web site is a comprehensive resource for parents and kids about substance abuse, depression, teen pregnancy, ADHD, suicide, delinquency, and much more.

Any comments? Contact us: comments@myreportlinks.com

Report Links

The Internet sites described below can be accessed at http://www.myreportlinks.com

▶ **Principles of Drug Addiction Treatment: A Research Based Guide**
Addicts often require repeat treatments in order to stay off drugs. The most effective approaches to treating drug addiction are discussed, as well as answers to frequently asked questions about addiction.

▶ **Street Terms: Drugs and the Drug Trade, Drug Type Cocaine**
This extensive collection of slang terms used by drug dealers and users to describe cocaine and the activities surrounding its use is a valuable resource for parents, teachers, and students.

▶ **Street Terms: Drugs and the Drug Trade, Drug Type Crack**
A valuable resource for parents, teachers, and students that discusses the use of crack, as well as street names for the drug.

▶ **Study Finds Significant Mental Deficits in Toddlers Exposed to Cocaine Before Birth**
You will learn about what happens to the mental capabilities of children who were exposed to cocaine in the womb.

▶ **Substance Abuse and Mental Health Services Administration**
At this Web site you will find information on national trends related to mental health services, addiction treatment, and substance abuse prevention. Statistical data, workplace resources, and a family guide to keeping youth, ages seven to eighteen, mentally healthy and drug free are included.

▶ **Tips for Teens: The Truth About Cocaine**
This site dispels some myths concerning cocaine and helps to give a clear picture of the effects, signs, and risks involved in using the drug.

▶ **Toxicity, Cocaine**
Learn about the history of cocaine abuse, the pharmacology of the drug, and its long-term medical effects by reading this in-depth article.

▶ **What's Up with Cocaine and Crack?**
Learn what cocaine and crack look like and where they come from. You will find information on how cocaine and crack are used, nicknames for these drugs, and the mental and physical effects they have on people.

Any comments? Contact us: comments@myreportlinks.com

Cocaine and Crack Facts

- Each year, more than three hundred thousand Americans try cocaine for the first time.

- In 2000, there were an estimated 2,707,000 chronic cocaine users and 3,035,000 occasional cocaine users in the United States.

- According to 2002 surveys, 3.6 percent of eighth graders and 7.8 percent of twelfth graders reported using cocaine at least once during their lifetimes.

- Users spent $35.3 billion on cocaine in 2000.

- Drug trafficking worldwide is a $400 billion per-year industry.

- Each year, drug traffickers attempt to smuggle more than 500 metric tons (492 long tons) of cocaine into the United States.

- More than 171,000 pounds (77,564 kilograms) of cocaine were seized nationally during fiscal year 2002.

- Approximately half of all crime in the United States is connected to drugs.

- According to a 1997 study, approximately 72 percent of state drug offenders were incarcerated for a cocaine offense.

- In fiscal year 2001, the average length of sentence received by federal crack cocaine offenders was nine years, seven months.

- In 2002, there were 199,198 reported mentions of cocaine in hospital emergency departments (emergency rooms). A drug mention refers to a substance that was recorded in a report during a visit to the emergency department.

- Between thirty thousand and fifty thousand babies are born each year to mothers who smoke crack during their pregnancies.

Chapter 1

STORIES OF COCAINE AND CRACK ABUSE

Darrell Porter was a baseball hero. He played in four Major League All-Star Games and was the MVP of the 1982 World Series for the Saint Louis Cardinals. Sadly, he was also addicted to cocaine.

Once, while high on coke, Porter brutally beat a man. Minutes later, he could not remember why he did. He spent most of one winter sitting in his house, clutching a shotgun. In a state of cocaine-induced paranoia, he was convinced that someone was out to get him.

"Ever since I started taking drugs I've been a cold-hearted person who doesn't give a flip about anything, except the way I feel," Porter wrote. "I've drifted away from my family and friends. . . . I hate drugs, and I hate what they've done to me. I can't cope with anything anymore. . . . I hate myself so much!"[1]

Porter preached against drugs through the Fellowship of Christian Athletes. No matter how hard he tried, he could not beat his addiction. On August 5, 2002—while high on cocaine—he smashed his car. He got out, wandered aimlessly, then dropped dead of heart failure. Cocaine had killed him.

Cocaine and crack have many street names. People use these as slang words so that nonusers might not know what they are talking about. On the street, cocaine has more than a hundred nicknames. They include: coke, C, snow, flake, blow, yay, rails, nose candy, toot, white, co-co puff, powder, fluff, sniff, and stuff. Crack's many nicknames include rock, rocky, wash, stones, base, big C, candy, carrie, and star burst.

Stories of Cocaine and Crack Abuse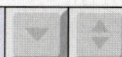

▲ Darrell Porter is shown here in his days playing for the Texas Rangers. A former World Series MVP, Porter ruined his life by abusing cocaine.

Many young people think they can handle cocaine. You cannot control cocaine, though. It almost always controls you.

Each year, more than three hundred thousand Americans try cocaine for the first time. Many are likely to join the more than 2 million other Americans who are addicted to cocaine. Addicts suffer from a variety of health problems: chronic headaches, irregular heartbeats, seizures, and strokes. Many who snort cocaine powder develop nosebleeds or infections as the coke burns away the lining of their nose. Many who smoke crack cocaine develop mouth sores and blackened lungs. Coke addicts can be surly, easy to anger, paranoid, and suicidal. They will lie, rob, and even kill for money to keep up their habit.

Many cocaine abusers damage more than just their own bodies. One year, an estimated three hundred thousand babies were born addicted to cocaine. These "crack babies" cry loudly and long. "They cry because they are in pain and suffering," said Nancy Shatz, a nurse at San Francisco General. "They don't even like to be touched."[2]

Cocaine does not discriminate. It ruins the lives of rich and poor. Here are a few of the millions of tragic stories related to cocaine:

▶ Yasmine Bleeth

In the mid-1990s, Yasmine Bleeth starred on the hit television show *Baywatch*. She was one of Hollywood's most beautiful celebrities. In 1997, she broke up with her boyfriend. Feeling low, she turned to cocaine. At first, Bleeth snorted coke socially. Three months later, she made her first call to a drug dealer. "It was all I could think about," she said. "When I was high, I didn't think about my problems. I had no pain. I wouldn't sleep for two or three days, sometimes even four or five."[3]

By 1999, Bleeth was a physical wreck. "I looked like an alien," she said. "My eyes were bulging out of my face. I was 110 pounds and a size 0. I looked dead."[4] An infection, caused by

Stories of Cocaine and Crack Abuse

In the 1990s, Yasmine Bleeth was an actress and model who starred in the series Baywatch. She is shown here in court after her arrest for cocaine possession in 2001.

snorting cocaine, festered in her nose. A doctor told her that the infection, if it had gone untreated, could have killed her. Despite the frightening news, she did not stop doing coke.

During the night of September 12, 2001, while high on cocaine, Bleeth crashed her car in Michigan and nearly died. From that moment, with the help of professionals and loved ones, Bleeth turned her life around. "I've proven to myself that I can't have both drugs and love," she said. "Every day, I have to make the choice again. So far, I choose love."[5]

Len Bias

Len Bias did not get to make such a choice. In the mid-1980s, Bias starred for the University of Maryland basketball team. A six-foot-eight-inch marvel, he possessed a chiseled physique and a soft jump shot. In 1985, Bias was named his conference's Player of the Year, beating out Michael Jordan. His coach, Lefty Driesell, called him "the greatest basketball player that ever played in the Atlantic Coast Conference."[6] In 1986, Bias was taken second overall in the NBA Draft by the Boston Celtics.

Yet Bias would never play a game in the NBA. On June 18, 1986, he and his buddies celebrated his getting drafted by drinking alcohol and snorting cocaine. He hung out with friends all night, then returned to his dorm room at 3:00 A.M. Three hours later, while talking to his roommate, his heart stopped beating, and soon he was dead.

Following Bias's death, friends and family insisted that he had tried cocaine only one time in his life. The lesson was unmistakable: Cocaine, taken just once, can kill you.

▶ Everyday People: Nadine*

In college, Nadine considered herself the "party queen." After studying and working all week, she felt she deserved to let loose on the weekends. She dressed up, went to parties, drank, and

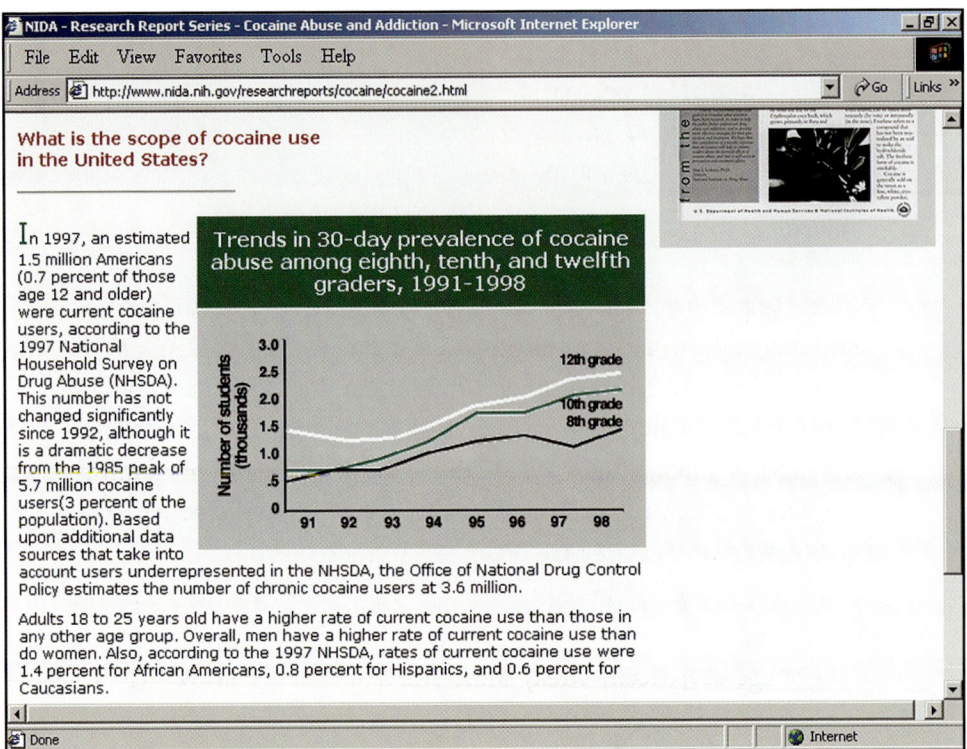

▲ This graph shows the number of young people who said they had done cocaine in the past thirty days at various times from 1991 to 1998. The number of users rose substantially over that period of time.

*Disclaimer: While the stories of abuse in this book are real, many of the names have been changed.

Stories of Cocaine and Crack Abuse

experimented with drugs. By the time she turned nineteen, her drug of choice was crack cocaine.

Soon all the money she made during the week was spent on white crystals. The "party queen" became a recluse. "I didn't care what I wore, if my hair was brushed, or even if I showered," she recalled. "All I thought of was a pipe filled with cocaine and where could I get more."

Nadine's habit took over her life. She lost her car, her job, her friends, and her chance for a college education. One morning, she stared at the items lying around the bathroom. "There was my old makeup bag, my curling iron, and a blow dryer," she said, "but I couldn't remember the last time I used any of them. . . . For a moment in time, I stood as a living ghost looking at the remains of a girl that had been dead for a couple of years."[7]

Several of Nadine's party friends wound up in prison. Others died. Nadine, who endured the pain of withdrawal and recovery, is now a member of a drug awareness group.

▶ Ricky

Marie hopes that her son, Ricky, will someday escape addiction. She relayed her story to an Internet site on March 27, 2003. Ricky, whom Marie called her "little angel," grew up in a loving family. His little brother adored him. Yet after he became addicted to crack, Ricky hurt himself and everyone in his family. He stole thousands of dollars from his mother, grandmother, and great-grandmother. When Marie prevented him from scoring crack by grounding him one evening, he threatened to stab her with a knife.

At age seventeen, Ricky stole Marie's car and drove off for good. His friends last saw him smoking crack in a dirty apartment. Marie called Ricky's situation a "long, sad miserable road."[8] It is a road of addiction and a path to destruction.

Chapter 2

HISTORY OF COCAINE AND CRACK

More than four thousand years ago, native people in the high mountain ranges of South America discovered they could chew the leaves of coca plants. Coca increased their oxygen intake and gave them more energy. They considered it a gift from God.

In the 1500s, Europeans discovered coca and brought it back to their continent. In the mid-1800s, a German scientist extracted cocaine from coca leaves. At first, doctors thought it was a miracle drug. Doctors prescribed it for everything from exhaustion to a cure for morphine addiction.

In 1863, a French company marketed Vin Mariani—a coca wine that even Roman Catholic Pope Leo XIII enjoyed. In the 1880s, doctors used cocaine as a local anesthetic in eye surgery. Legendary psychiatrist Sigmund Freud trumpeted the benefits of the new drug. "I take very small doses of it regularly and against depression and against indigestion, and with the most brilliant success," he wrote.[1] One of Freud's patients later died from cocaine overdose, but the drug grew in popularity. In 1886, Coca-Cola, a soft drink with coca as an ingredient, became a new American craze.

▶ Cocaine in America

After the turn of the century, people began to snort cocaine powder. Soon, Americans became aware of the drug's harmful effects. The Coca-Cola Company removed coca from its formula. In 1912, the United Sates government reported five thousand cocaine-related fatalities in one year. In 1914, the Harrison Narcotics Act banned the drug in the United States.

History of Cocaine and Crack

▲ Native peoples in South America would chew coca leaves to give them energy. Coca leaves are the natural ingredient from which cocaine is made.

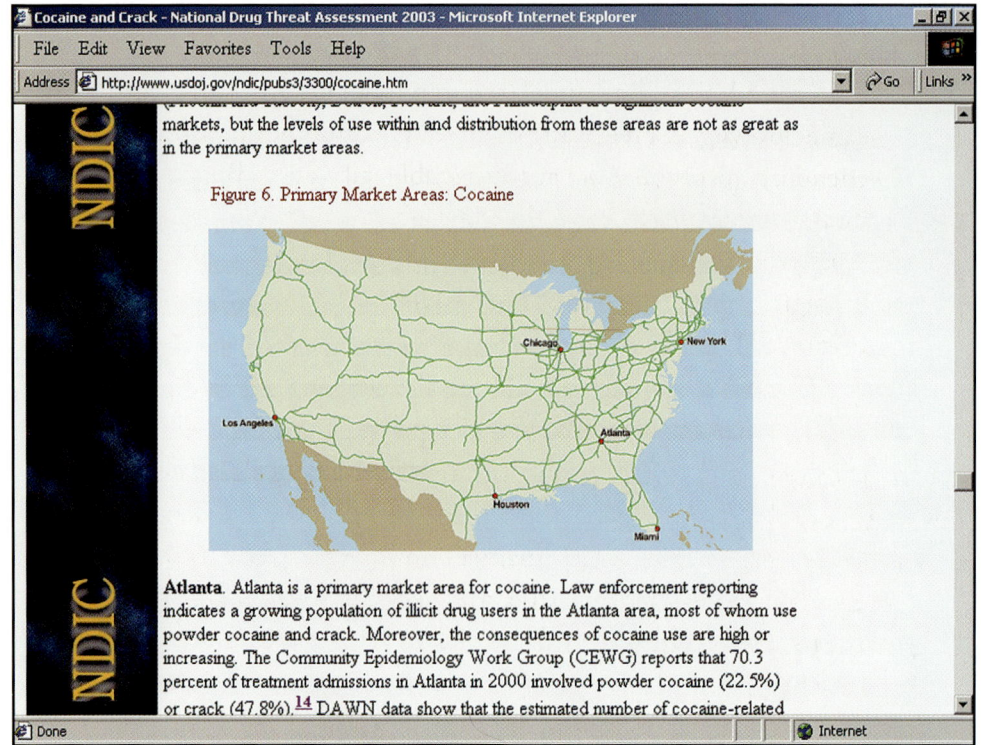

▲ This map shows the major markets for cocaine in the United States in 2000, and the major routes that drug traffickers use to transport it. As law enforcement cuts off certain routes, the drug traffickers try to create new ones.

For decades thereafter, few Americans tried cocaine. It remained popular only among certain small groups, such as jazz musicians, actors, and artists. In the 1970s, however, rock musicians were known to use cocaine. Soon, its popularity exploded. Coke became the drug of choice among rich, urban professionals, who were among the few who could afford the pricey drug. In 1981, the wholesale price for a kilogram (2.2 pounds) of cocaine was fifty-five thousand dollars.

There was a great demand for cocaine. South American drug gangs increased their production of the drug. The wholesale price for a kilo of coke dropped to twenty-five thousand dollars in 1984. Teenagers across the United States became fascinated with the white powder—and addicted to it. A study in the mid-1980s found that 17 percent of American teens had tried cocaine.

Around the same time, the more-potent freebase cocaine came into vogue. Freebasing involved cooking cocaine with other chemicals to produce a hard, smokable substance. Because freebasing was dangerous and time consuming, it was not suited for mass production. Drug dealers, though, liked the idea of a "higher high." Thus, they produced something similar to freebase cocaine. They created a smokable substance called crack.

The Crack Epidemic

By the 1980s, crack became affordable for the common person. "Rocks" of crack were sold for less than ten dollars. In fact, drug dealers discovered a new market: unsupervised and vulnerable inner-city kids—mostly African Americans—who wandered the streets. Dealers pushed it; kids took it. They were hooked. Drug cartels in South America expanded to meet the demand. Peru, for example, increased its coca production from 5,442 tons in 1980 to more than 250,000 tons in 1991.

Throughout the middle and late 1980s, a crack epidemic plagued America's cities. Drug dealers took over run-down homes to cook cocaine in, which they then called crack houses. Groups of "crackheads"—adults, teens, and even children who were addicted to crack—could be found in almost every neighborhood. "It hits the weakest part of the neighborhood first," said Miami police spokesperson Delrish Moss, "and then, like a cancer, it spreads."[2]

Addicts did anything to support their habit. They sold drugs themselves, stole, and killed. Women, even young girls, turned to prostitution for drug money. Thousands of female addicts gave birth to "crack babies." These babies suffered painful withdrawal symptoms and severe health problems. Sometimes, the crack-addicted mothers left their babies at the hospital and never came back.

MyReportLinks.com Books

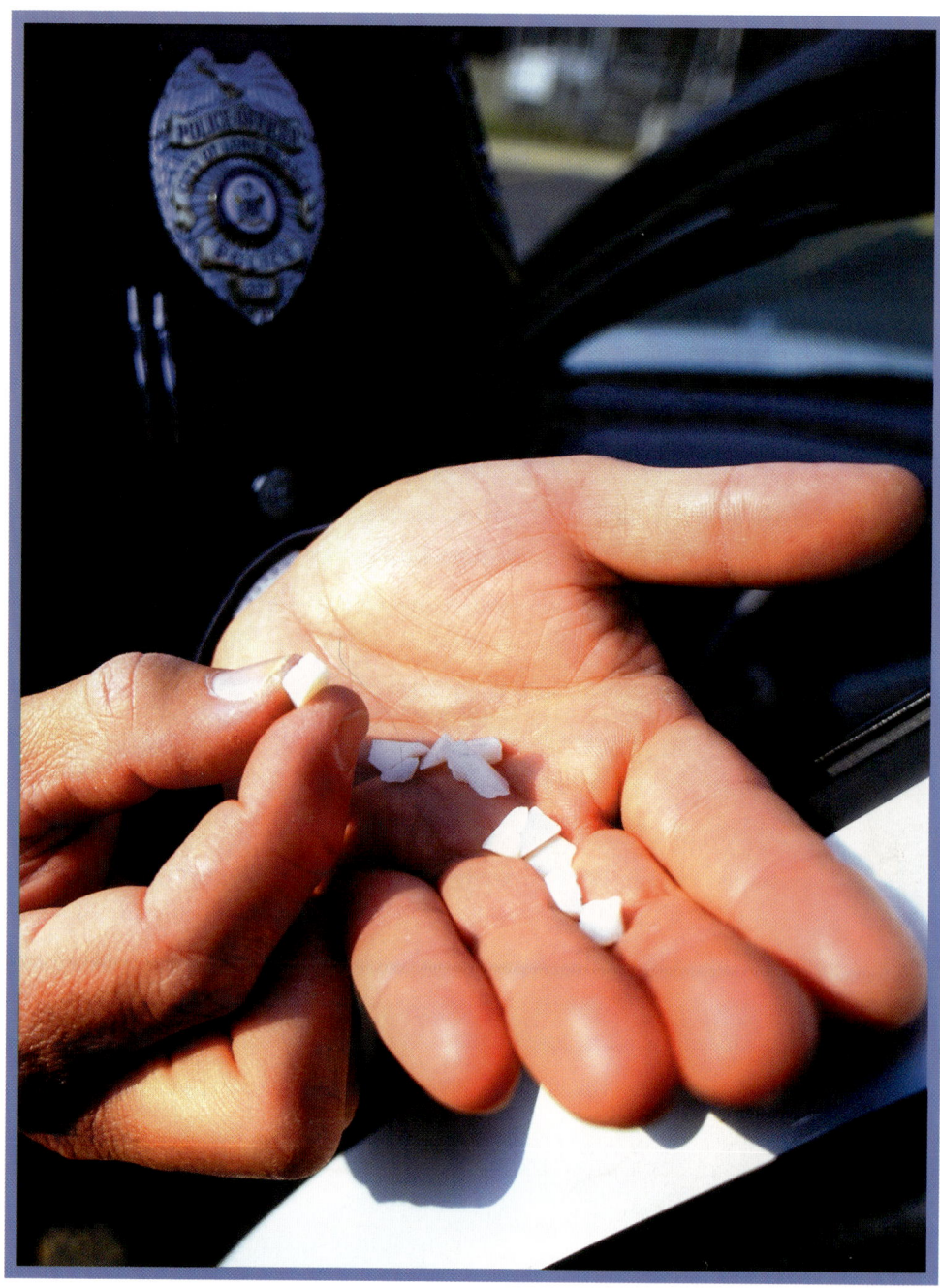

▲ This police officer is holding rocks of crack. Crack became a major problem in the United States in the 1980s. Drug abusers used the drug because it was basically a cheaper form of cocaine.

Moreover, many kids were lured by the power and money of selling crack. Dealers carried guns, even assault weapons, and some neighborhoods resembled war zones. Many people were killed in drug-related shootings. These victims included innocent bystanders—sometimes children.

Federal officials responded with a "war on drugs." They spent billions of dollars to tackle the problem. In 1986, lawmakers imposed a mandatory five-year sentence for anyone possessing five grams of crack. Convicted drug users swelled America's prisons. In a *New York Times*/CBS News poll in September 1989, 65 percent of Americans selected "drugs" as the number-one problem facing the nation.

Crack use subsided somewhat in the 1990s, largely because the stiff sentences scared away drug dealers. In Washington, D.C., murders, many drug related, dropped from 482 in 1991 to 241 in 2001. However, cocaine and crack use still remained high. In

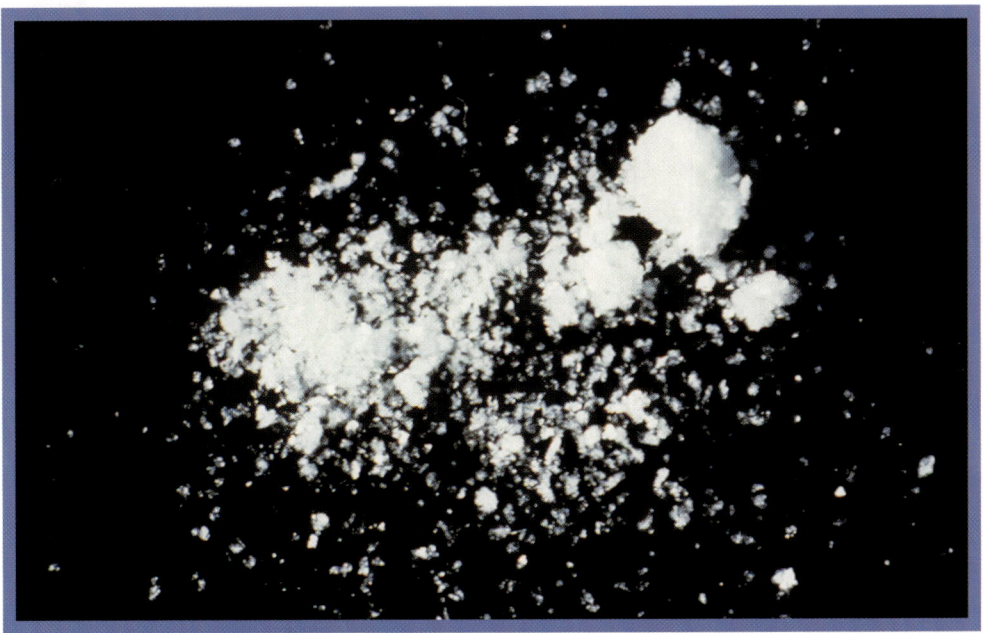

▲ In the ten-year period from 1991 to 2001, the use of crack slightly declined. Crack, though, is still a problem facing drug abuse counselors and law enforcement officials.

PERCENTAGE OF AMERICANS REPORTING LIFETIME USE OF CRACK BY AGE GROUP, 2002

AGE GROUP	LIFETIME	PAST YEAR	PAST MONTH
12–17	0.7%	0.4%	0.1%
18–25	3.8%	0.9%	0.2%
26 and older	3.9%	0.7%	0.3%
Total population	3.6%	0.7%	0.2%

Source: National Survey on Drug Use and Health

2000, hospitals experienced more medical emergencies related to cocaine than any other drug.

Today, cocaine and crack are among a growing number of drugs that plague America. An estimated 8 million children have a parent who is addicted to drugs or alcohol.[3] Moreover, studies show that 70 percent of addicts' children become addicts themselves.[4] The grip of cocaine and crack is ferociously powerful. Only by never trying them can one be absolutely sure to avoid their grasp.

Chapter 3

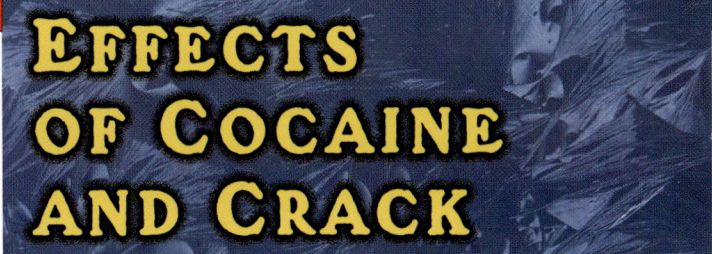

EFFECTS OF COCAINE AND CRACK

Cocaine is an alkaloid, meaning it is from the same family as such addictive chemicals as nicotine and caffeine. While smoking cigarettes and drinking too much coffee can be harmful, ingesting cocaine is much worse. It wreaks havoc on the body and can be deadly.

▶ Forms of Cocaine

Cocaine is purchased in the form of white powder, although that powder may not be pure cocaine. Dealers often "cut" (dilute) the powder with such substances as sugar and baking soda. Sometimes they mix in other dangerous drugs, such as heroin.

Users have several options for ingesting cocaine. They can inhale the powder through their nose. They can mix it with water and inject it with a needle or syringe into a vein. Or they can cook the powder with other chemicals to make freebase or crack cocaine, then smoke the hardened substance. The three forms produce different highs—and different dangers.

Snorting cocaine powder is one way to use the drug. Snorted

Cocaine is most commonly ingested by snorting its powder form.

▶ 23 ◀

cocaine takes a few minutes to reach the brain. The user will reach a peak high in about fifteen minutes. When it is injected into a vein, the drug reaches the brain more quickly and creates a stronger "rush."

Freebase cocaine became popular in the 1970s, as users heard that the derived drug created a better high. Freebasing is a complicated and risky process. It involves mixing and cooking cocaine powder with potentially explosive solvents. Entertainer Richard Pryor is one of the many who has badly burned himself trying to freebase.

Crack cocaine is easier to make than freebase cocaine. It involves mixing cocaine with common substances to create a paste that eventually hardens. The user then smokes the "rock" in a pipe. He or she will experience a high within seconds, although it lasts only about fifteen minutes—much shorter than with snorted cocaine. A crack user often compensates for the short high by taking more "hits."

Effects on the Brain

The brain contains a neurotransmitter (a chemical) called dopamine, which is critical to a person's well-being. Dopamine affects a person's mood, thinking ability, body movements, and experiences of pleasure. When cocaine enters the brain, it causes a large amount of dopamine to be released into synapses in the brain's "pleasure center." Indeed, the release of dopamine makes the body feel a great deal of pleasure. Cocaine also prevents dopamine from leaving the synapses, meaning the pleasurable feelings last a long time.

It would be nice if dopamine levels returned to normal once the high was over, but they do not. Cocaine actually damages the brain's ability to produce the proper amount of dopamine. This causes the user's mood to "crash." The person becomes irritable, tired, and depressed. The brain craves more dopamine, but—because of the damage the drug has caused—the brain cannot

▶ Effects of Cocaine and Crack

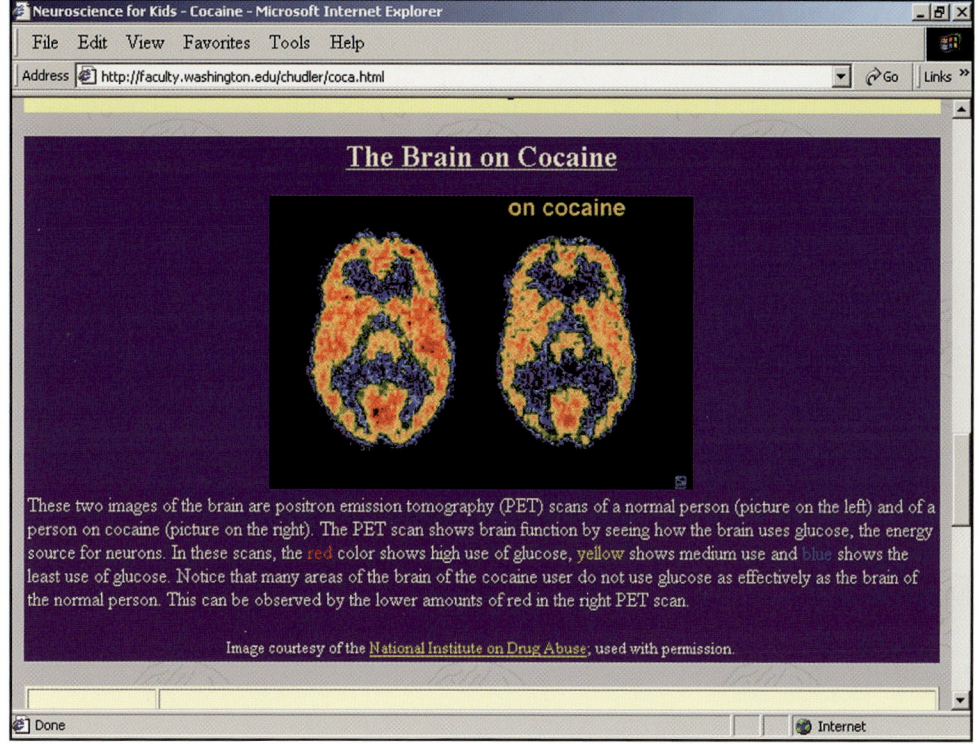

▲ Cocaine affects the brain by releasing dopamine into the brain's pleasure center. The brain then needs cocaine to satisfy the need to reach the same level of euphoria.

make enough dopamine on its own. It needs more cocaine to trigger the release of the dopamine. The user then satisfies this craving by taking more of the drug. It is all part of a vicious cycle called addiction.

Cocaine also interacts with other neurotransmitters, including norepinephrine and serotonin. Scientists are still exploring how cocaine's interaction with those neurotransmitters affects the brain and the body. In addition, cocaine affects other parts of the brain besides the "pleasure center." It affects the prefrontal cortex and amygdala, which are involved in memory and learning.

▶ Short-Term Effects

A small amount of cocaine makes a user feel "wired." For minutes or hours, he or she is euphoric, energetic, often very talkative. The person may feel irritable and anxious. His or her sensations of touch, sight, and sound are more pronounced. The person often feels wide awake, mentally alert, and not hungry. Cocaine use produces dramatic effects on the body. The user experiences dilated pupils and increased heart rate, blood pressure, and body temperature. Also, his or her blood vessels constrict, which reduces the flow of blood and oxygen to the heart.

The intake of large amounts of cocaine (several hundred milligrams) may lead to erratic and violent behavior. Users could

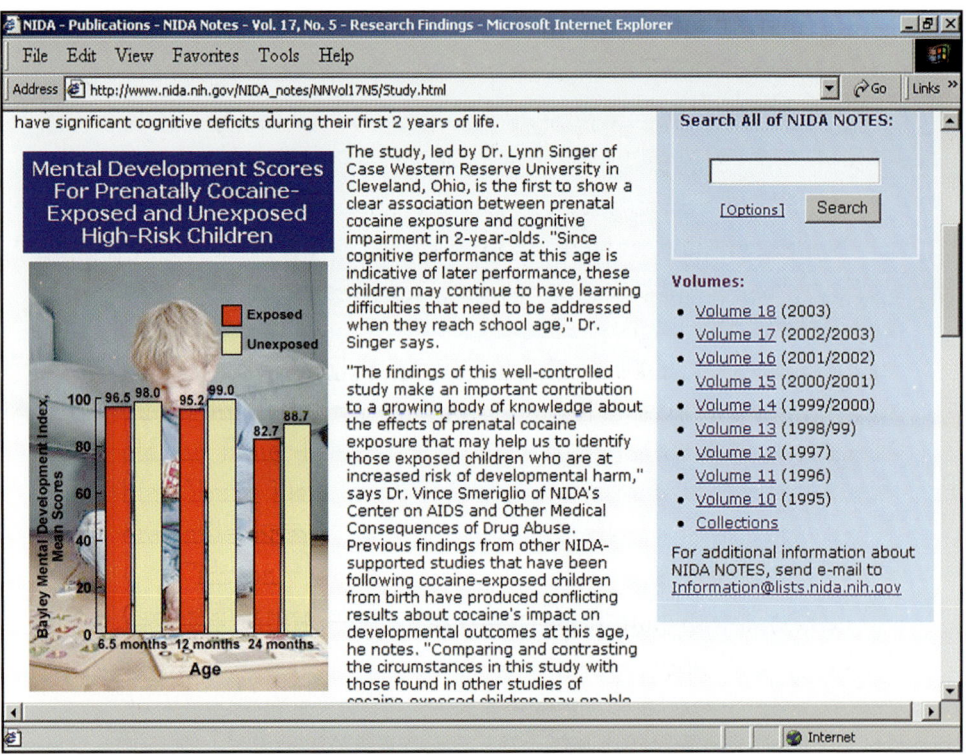

▲ This graph shows that women who used cocaine while pregnant often harmed the newborn baby's ability to develop as quickly as other children.

experience tremors, muscle twitches, and paranoia. Some suffer a seizure or a heart attack, which could be fatal.

▶ Long-Term Physical Effects

Cocaine is a sinister drug. It causes a person to crave it—to be addicted—after just one use. After repeated use, the user needs to take a larger amount of cocaine to reach a peak high. The larger the dose, the greater the damage to the body.

Repeated cocaine use damages the body severely. It harms the gastrointestinal, cardiovascular, respiratory, and neurological systems. One could suffer nausea and stomach pain, chaotic heart rhythms, and perhaps a heart attack. Since cocaine causes a loss of appetite and mood abnormalities, a user can become malnourished. The user might experience chest pain as well as chronic headaches, a seizure, or a stroke.

The intake of cocaine leads to other physical problems. Those who snort cocaine regularly may suffer from chronic runny noses and nosebleeds and have trouble smelling and swallowing. Users who take the drug intravenously can suffer infections or allergic reactions. Sharing needles means one could contract HIV. Smoking crack cocaine often results in sores or blisters on the lips. The smoke damages the lungs.

Those who take cocaine and alcohol simultaneously are also risking their lives. The two combine to create cocaethylene, which is highly toxic.

▶ Psychological Effects

Cocaine affects the mood and behavior of the addict—often in disturbing and ugly ways. Between uses, the person can suffer from irritability, restlessness, and depression. Some reach a state of paranoid psychosis, in which they experience auditory hallucinations (they hear voices).

A cocaine addict becomes obsessed with obtaining his or her next high. He or she loses interest in work or school. The person's

MyReportLinks.com Books

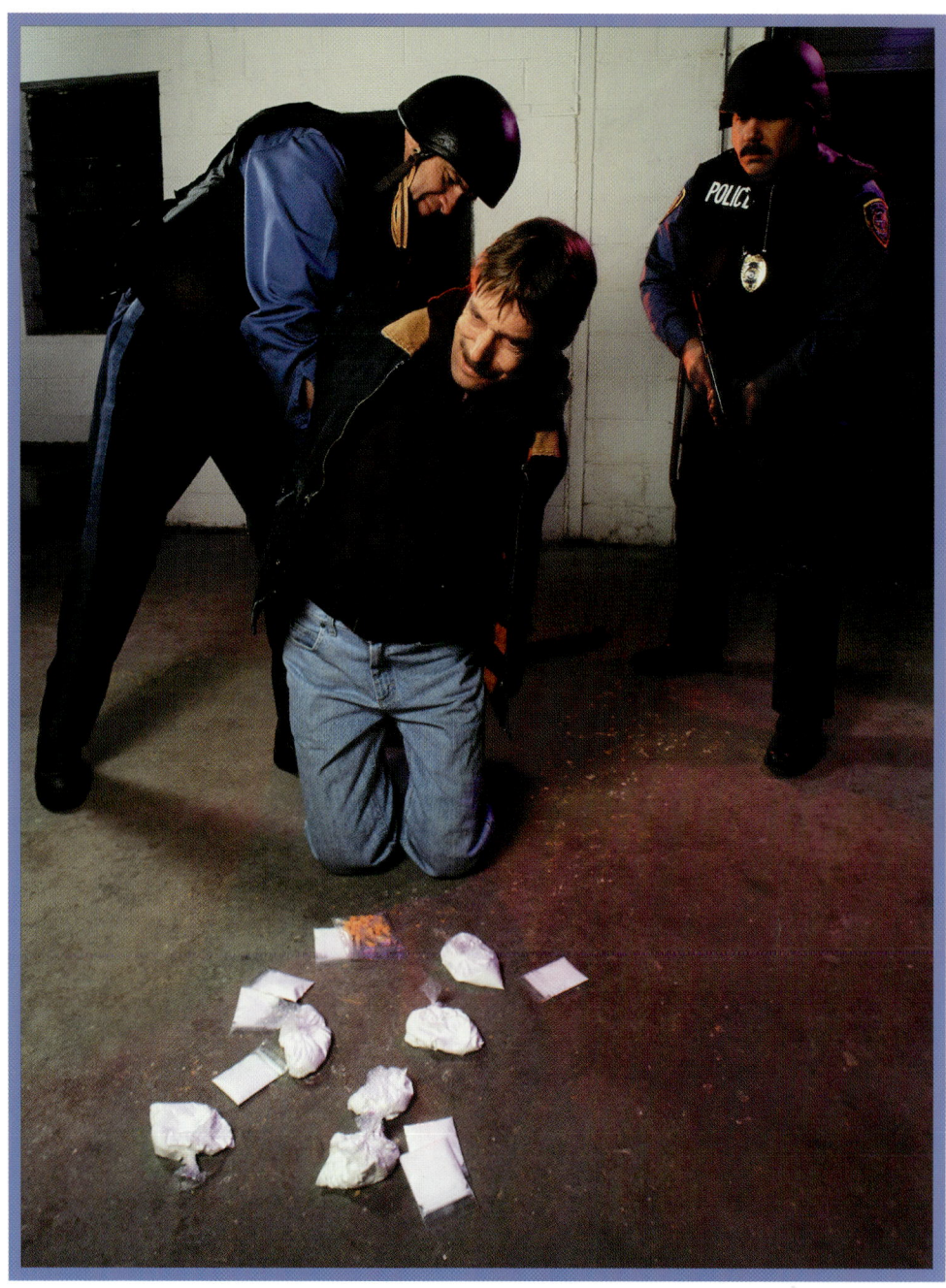

▲ Cocaine is an expensive habit. Oftentimes cocaine abusers will turn to crime in order to get money to buy more drugs. Sometimes they will become drug dealers themselves.

Effects of Cocaine and Crack

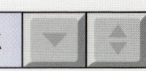

mood is unstable; he or she could become surly or perhaps volatile. The user will often become hostile to friends and loved ones—and perhaps shut them out of his or her life. To obtain money to buy more coke, the user might commit immoral or illegal acts. He or she might steal from friends or family—or rob a stranger. He or she might physically assault someone or even kill the person for drug money.

Hitting Bottom

Ronnie is an example of an addict who plummeted to the lowest of depths. In high school, Ronnie was a good student and captain of the track team. Around that time, he started to use drugs and drink heavily. He not only quit the track team, but he also quit school. He worked dead-end jobs to get by, and he often slept in the homes of buddies—from whom he stole. Running out of friends, Ronnie moved in with his mother and stole from her, too. In time, he crashed at the homes of other drug addicts—people he did not even know—and sometimes slept on the streets. Ronnie reached a point where he no longer wanted to live. He attempted suicide, overdosing on aspirin. He wound up in a psychiatric ward, where his father begged him to seek professional help for his addiction. He graduated from a drug rehab program in 2002.[1]

29

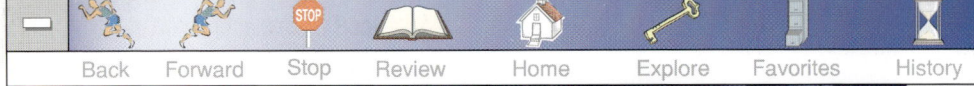

Chapter 4 ▶

PRODUCING AND SELLING COCAINE AND CRACK

To some people, drug dealing is a despicable crime. To others, it is an irresistible way to make money. Drug trafficking is a $400-billion-per-year industry, representing 8 percent of the world's trade. Americans alone spend tens of billions of dollars per year on cocaine and crack.

▲ *Most of the coca leaves that are processed into cocaine are grown in Peru. The processing is often done in Colombia.*

▶ Producing and Selling Cocaine and Crack

STREET NAMES FOR CRACK AND COCAINE

DRUG	STREET NAMES
Cocaine	All American drug, Aspirin, Barbs, Bernie, Blow, C, Candy sugar, Coca, Coke, Co-co Puff, Double bubble, Flake, Flave, Florida snow, Fluff, Foo foo, Gin, Gold dust, Happy dust, Icing, Jelly, Lady, Mama coca, Mojo, Nose candy, Nose stuff, Oyster stew, Paradise, Pariba, Pearl, Powder, Rails, Scorpion, Sevenup, Sniff, Snow, Snow white, Stuff, Sugar boogers, Toot, White, Yay, Zip
Crack	Basa, Base, Big C, Black rock, Candy, Carrie, Cds, Electric Kool-Aid, Real tops, Rock, Rocks, Rocky, Roxanne, Star Burst, Stones, Twinkle, Wash, Yam

Source: Office of National Drug Control Policy

Drug traffickers risk imprisonment and death every day of their lives. Yet they cannot resist the lure of big money. Pablo Escobar, the "godfather" of drug trafficking in Colombia, accumulated a net worth of about $3 billion. A war between him and the Colombian government led to four thousand deaths. Escobar was sent to prison in 1991, but he eventually escaped. On December 2, 1993, he was hunted down by Colombian security forces and shot to death. Colombian prosecutor General Gustavo de Greiff said, "Let this be a lesson to all criminals that sooner or later we will catch them."[1]

▶ Making and Selling Cocaine

Most cocaine originates in Peru, a nation in South America. Peru is a poor country in which millions of people struggle to make a living. Desperate for a decent wage, thousands work in coca fields harvesting the plants that will become cocaine. At its peak in 1992, Peruvians harvested 315,000 acres (127,575 hectares) for coca. After Peru, Colombia and Bolivia are the largest producers of the notorious plant.

After harvesting coca leaves, villagers haul them to refining tanks. Many of these tanks are merely empty swimming pools. At this stage, coca is refined into a paste. When about a ton of coca paste is produced, it is shipped via airplane to the final processing centers. Most of these centers are in Colombia, a country controlled largely by powerful drug cartels. In clandestine laboratories, coca paste is transformed into cocaine powder.

The powder is then smuggled into the United States and other countries that demand the drug. To do so, the Colombian drug lords have created a complex network of dealers and routes. Dealers smuggle the drug via commercial airplanes and private

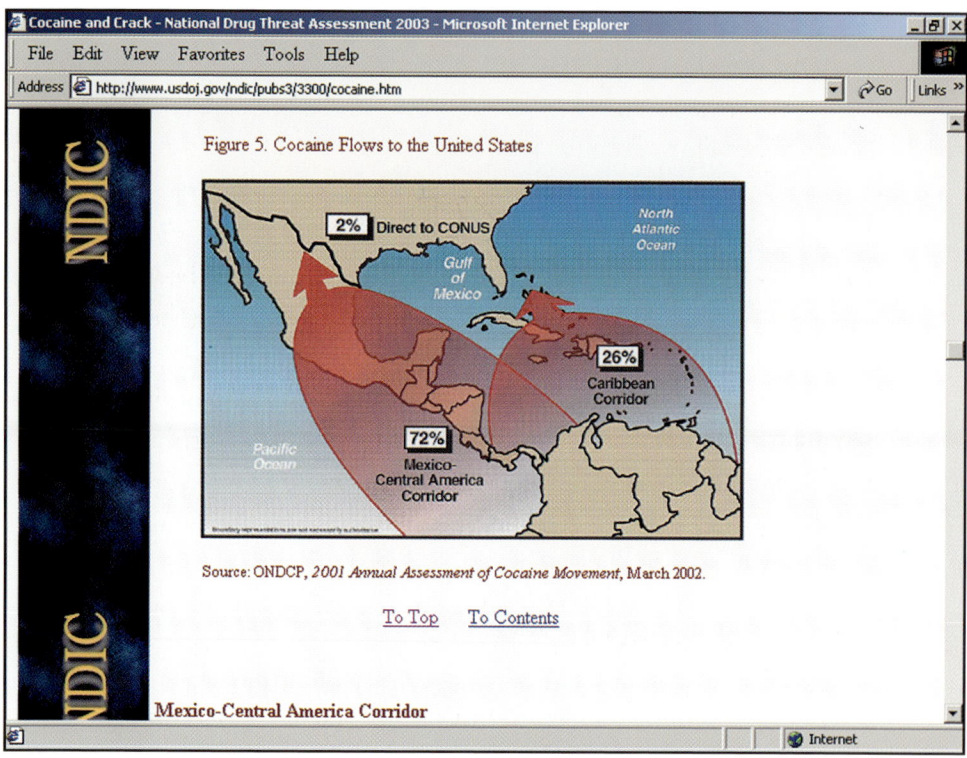

▲ This figure shows where the cocaine that reaches the United States comes from. The two major routes are from western South America through Mexico, or from eastern South America through the Caribbean islands.

▶ Producing and Selling Cocaine and Crack

Law enforcement officials and attorneys aggressively prosecute drug cases. Penalties for selling drugs like cocaine increase if it is done near a school where young people are often present.

planes. They also drive it up through Mexico, or they smuggle it in on boats.

Each year, more than 550 tons (500 metric tons) of cocaine flow into the United States. Some of this is seized by law enforcement, but most slips through. Most of that cocaine is smuggled across the United States' southwest border.

Since the 1990s, Mexican traffickers have become heavily involved in cocaine smuggling. In exchange for trafficking cocaine for the Colombians, they receive part of that cocaine as payment. Traffickers in Mexico now control cocaine distribution to the western and midwestern United States. Colombians control the East. The Colombian and Mexican drug networks have "cells" in many major American cities. Each cell performs a specific function—transportation, local distribution, or money movement. Managers in Colombia oversee the operation.

The cells frequently sell cocaine to the leaders of street gangs. Gang leaders push cocaine and crack on gang members. Also, gang leaders and members are often the ones who transform cocaine powder into crack. Gang members often use crack and/or "push" it to others on the street. In recent years, gangs have expanded their drug operations from major cities to smaller urban cities. Some gang members in Seattle, Washington, for example, relocated to nearby Spokane to peddle crack.

Crack rocks are tiny, ranging from one-tenth to one-half of a gram. They are usually packaged in vials, sealed bags, or film canisters. A rock can sell for anywhere from three dollars up to fifty dollars, but ten dollars to twenty dollars is the normal rate.

▶ Corrupting Communities

Armed with cocaine or crack, street dealers cannot wait to make their next sale. They may sell the drug at their home, at crack houses, at clubs, and even on school grounds. Some hang out at crowded bus or subway stations where drug seekers know to find them.

Some drug dealers like to prey on children. They offer kids crack for a low price or for free, claiming it is a really special treat. Some of these kids go back to the dealer for more crack. They become young addicts—and steady customers for the dealer as a child's need for the drug increases.

Chapter 5

Avoiding Drugs and Getting Help

It is not easy being a teenager. A teen's body transforms from a child's to an adult's—whether he or she wants it to or not. Hormones make teenagers more emotional. They might feel angry, depressed, confused, or even invincible. It is often in these

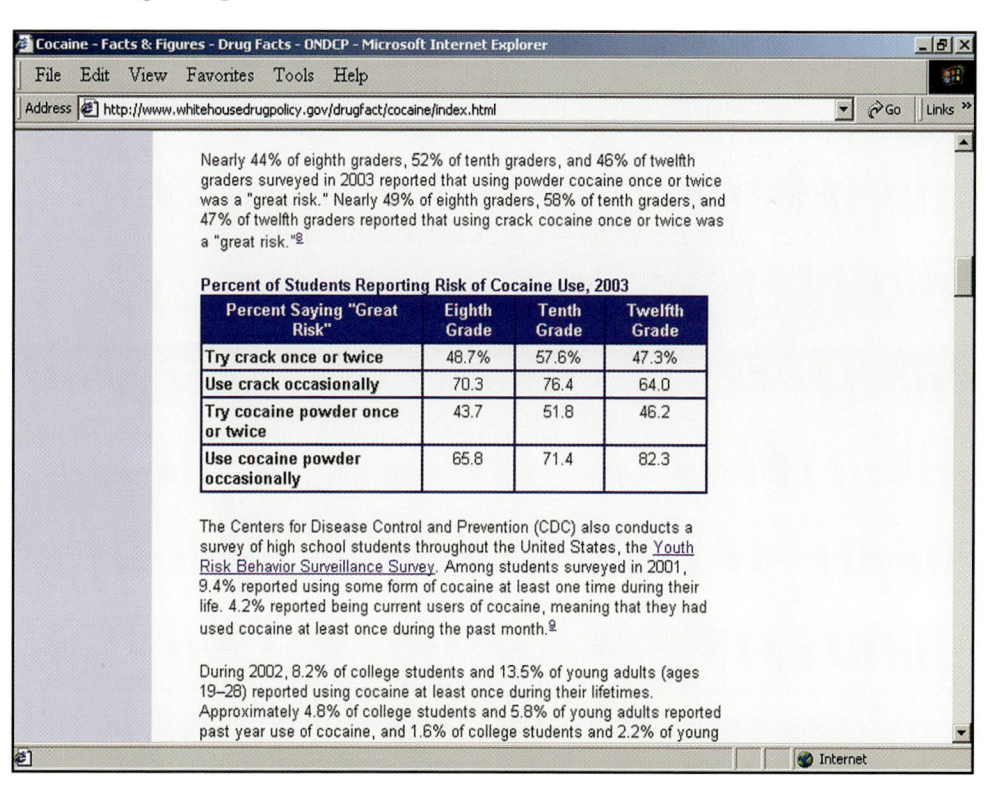

Nearly 44% of eighth graders, 52% of tenth graders, and 46% of twelfth graders surveyed in 2003 reported that using powder cocaine once or twice was a "great risk." Nearly 49% of eighth graders, 58% of tenth graders, and 47% of twelfth graders reported that using crack cocaine once or twice was a "great risk."[8]

Percent of Students Reporting Risk of Cocaine Use, 2003

Percent Saying "Great Risk"	Eighth Grade	Tenth Grade	Twelfth Grade
Try crack once or twice	48.7%	57.6%	47.3%
Use crack occasionally	70.3	76.4	64.0
Try cocaine powder once or twice	43.7	51.8	46.2
Use cocaine powder occasionally	65.8	71.4	82.3

The Centers for Disease Control and Prevention (CDC) also conducts a survey of high school students throughout the United States, the Youth Risk Behavior Surveillance Survey. Among students surveyed in 2001, 9.4% reported using some form of cocaine at least one time during their life. 4.2% reported being current users of cocaine, meaning that they had used cocaine at least once during the past month.[9]

During 2002, 8.2% of college students and 13.5% of young adults (ages 19–28) reported using cocaine at least once during their lifetimes. Approximately 4.8% of college students and 5.8% of young adults reported past year use of cocaine, and 1.6% of college students and 2.2% of young

▲ Parents, teachers, and government officials are trying to get the message out that cocaine use can be extremely harmful. In 2003, only 48.7 percent of eighth graders, 57.6 percent of tenth graders, and 47.3 percent of twelfth graders felt that trying cocaine once or twice would be a "great risk."

PERCENTAGE OF AMERICANS REPORTING COCAINE USE, 2001–2002

GRADE	LIFETIME		PAST YEAR		PAST MONTH	
YEAR	2001	2002	2001	2002	2001	2002
8th	4.3%	3.6%	2.5%	2.3%	1.2%	1.1%
10th	5.7%	6.1%	3.6%	4.0%	1.3%	1.6%
12th	8.2%	7.8%	4.8%	5.0%	2.1%	2.3%

Source: Monitoring the Future Study

emotional states that many teenagers, without thinking rationally, begin taking drugs.

Other teens, feeling unsure of themselves, measure their worth by how "cool" their group of friends is. This means they will do anything—even drugs—to fit in. Also, many teenagers have great passion, and a powerful urge for excitement. Seeking a new thrill, many turn to drugs.

All of these reasons for drug use are reflected in national polls. When asked why they take drugs, young people typically give these responses:

- ✓ To be cool
- ✓ Because friends take them
- ✓ To feel good
- ✓ To relieve stress

When it comes to using cocaine, no reasons are good ones. Is it "cool" to become an addict—withdrawn, sickly, surly? Would a real "friend" want to jeopardize your health and future? Does it "feel good" to have nose infections, lip sores, or any of the numerous internal problems that cocaine causes? Does it "relieve stress" to be frantically craving your next hit day after day?

There are no good reasons to try cocaine, but there are plenty of reasons to avoid it. Cocaine can damage every organ of your body and even kill you. Just one hit can addict you for life. It is expensive, causing people to commit crimes to afford their habit. You could be suspended or expelled from sports teams, social clubs, and even school for using drugs. If caught by police, you could be arrested and imprisoned. The lesson is unmistakable: Cocaine ruins lives.

▶ Warning Signs

Cocaine addiction is powerful and can seldom be conquered alone. If you have an addiction, you must seek help. If a friend or loved one is addicted, he or she needs support.

Many people who try cocaine once or several times believe they have the willpower to stop when they want to. This is a mistake, and a potentially tragic one. If you have taken cocaine or crack once, it is imperative that you never try it again. If you have tried it two or more times, you are becoming addicted. You need to seek help.

Often it is hard to tell if friends or loved ones have a drug problem. One reason is that they usually try to hide their drug secret. Despite their deception, drug abusers give off certain warning signs that they have a problem. They might exhibit physical signs, such as a runny nose, sores on their lips, or red-rimmed eyes. They might become withdrawn, skip classes, and quit activities. They might ask you to loan them money. They might hound, beg, or even threaten you for cash. Serious cocaine abusers tend to lose weight, look sickly, or seem agitated, violent, or depressed. At this point, their life is in danger. You can help.

▶ Where to Go for Help

If you or someone you care about has a drug problem, you should discuss it with an adult you can trust. This may be a parent or a relative. It could also be a teacher, a coach, or your doctor. Often it is wise to talk to your school counselor, who likely is trained to handle such matters. Sometimes drug abusers are too nervous or ashamed to discuss their problem with people they know. Even for them, help is available.

Those seeking help with addiction can call Cocaine Anonymous or visit their Web site. "The only requirement for membership," states the site, "is a desire to stop using cocaine and all other mind-altering substances."[1] NAADAC is another alternative. It boasts the nation's largest network of alcoholism and drug-abuse treatment professionals. Some of the Web sites at the front of this book, and phone numbers in the back, can give you a good start if you are seeking help.

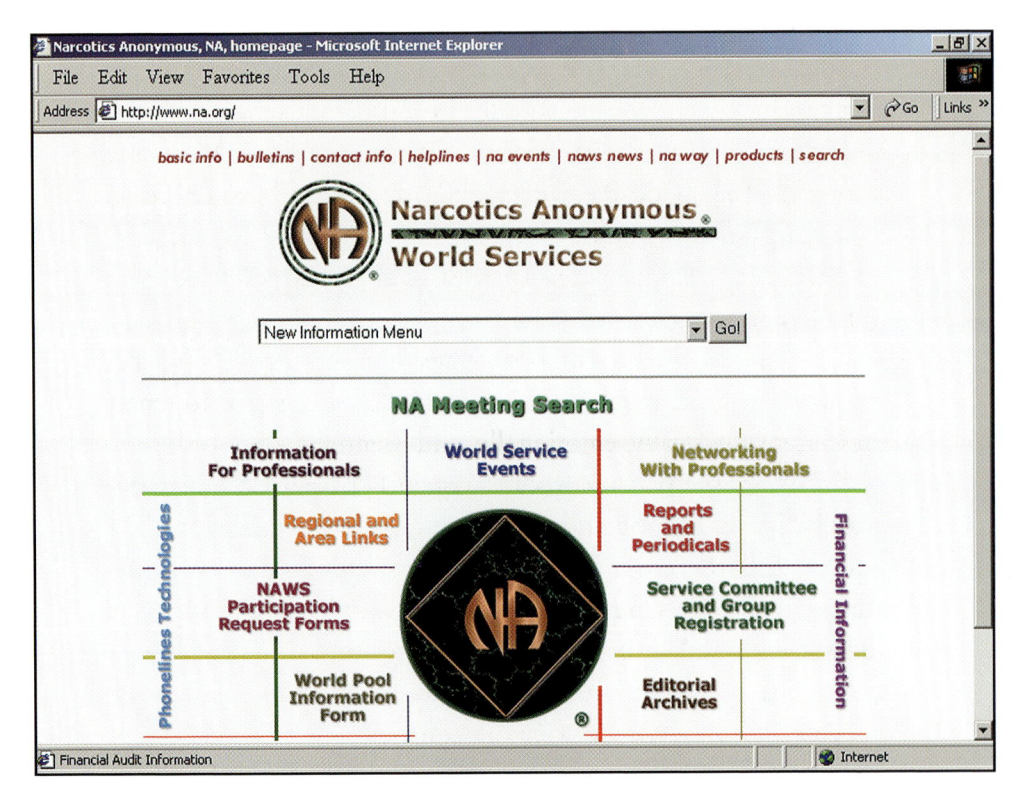

▲ Organizations such as Narcotics Anonymous (commonly called NA) exist to provide a place where people can go to get the help they need to stay off cocaine and other drugs.

Those seeking help with addiction should also check their phone book. It might list a local drug treatment center, a walk-in medical clinic, or a crisis center. You can also call your local hospital and ask how they can help you. Help is available, and it is not hard to find.

Treatment for Addiction

What can a patient expect when he goes for treatment for drug abuse? For one thing, he will receive a medical examination. If drugs have harmed his body, those ailments will be treated. It should be noted that many cocaine addicts have a coexisting mental disorder, such as depression or attention deficit disorder. These conditions should be evaluated and treated.

The first step in breaking addiction is to rid the body of the toxic substances. This usually occurs in a supervised medical setting called "detox." Going through cocaine withdrawal in detox is an intensely difficult process, but it is the only way to break free from the drug. Cocaine withdrawal sometimes lasts for days. Symptoms include intense craving for the drug, anxiety, irritability, depression, fatigue, anger, nausea, shaking, muscle pain, and difficulty sleeping.

Once detox is over, the patient needs to go through "rehab" at a drug treatment center. The goal at such a center is to repair the patient physically, emotionally, and mentally.

In rehab, the patient needs to regain her health. She will eat healthy meals and begin to exercise—perhaps starting with a walk around the grounds. She will also undergo individual and group counseling. Counselors will try to help her understand her addiction and allow her to express her feelings. In group counseling, she will realize that she is not alone—that others are fighting the same demons. Family counseling is often extremely important. Recovering addicts and their loved ones need to mend the ties that cocaine destroyed. Tears are often shed in these emotional meetings.

MyReportLinks.com Books

▲ Sometimes users need to attend drug treatment centers, where they will try to learn ways to avoid the craving for cocaine.

A standard rehab program is thirty days, but that is not enough to permanently beat addiction. Many recovering addicts find help at extended-care drug treatment centers. Others undergo twelve-step programs, similar to Alcoholics Anonymous, while others check into halfway houses. A halfway house is a place where recovering addicts can live and continue to receive treatment while they look for jobs and try to put their lives back in order.

In all of these programs, recovering addicts learn how to resist drugs and maintain a healthy lifestyle. They learn how to cope with their addiction and how to avoid situations in which they are likely to use cocaine. They may be put on a voucher-based system: If they remain drug free, they will receive points, which they can exchange for a reward, such as a ticket to a movie. This may seem simplistic, but it is a step in the right direction. Recovering addicts need all the help they can get in their long, hard road to recovery.

Drug Prevention

At points in your life, cocaine, crack, or other drugs of abuse may be an arm's length away from you. Your loved ones may not be there to stop you. Friends or dealers might even push you to take a hit, sniff a line, or pop a pill.

What will you do?

Ultimately, taking drugs is your decision. No one can stop you. However, since drugs are so frightfully dangerous, you should know what you would be getting yourself into. After all, would you consume a prescription drug without first reading the label? Educate yourself on the effects of cocaine and crack. Refer to the Web sites listed in the beginning of this book, or explore the books at your school or local library.

If the issue is bothering you, discuss drug use with your friends. You will probably find that they are against drugs, too, and you can support each other if one of you is feeling pressured.

In fact, did you know that more than 90 percent of teenagers do not take drugs? Among the vast majority of teens, drugs are definitely not cool.

If you find that your friends want you to take drugs, perhaps it is time to find new friends. A person who pushes drugs on you is unconcerned with your well-being. Is their friendship more important to you than your health, your future, your dreams?

Life offers plenty of natural highs for young people. Teenagers can Rollerblade and skateboard, swim and ski. They can joke with their friends, date, and dance. They can join clubs and play team sports. They can find expression in writing and acting, or music and singing.

▲ Drug courts such as this one are used to prosecute drug traffickers. Cocaine use can lead to health problems, death, poverty, and even years behind bars in a federal prison.

▶ Avoiding Drugs and Getting Help

▲ *Cocaine is usually ingested in its powder form. Yet no matter what type of cocaine a user abuses, its effects can be extremely harmful.*

Darrell Porter found joy in baseball, his family, and his friends. Cocaine led only to despair and an early death. "[Y]ou don't have to try drugs to know their effects," Porter wrote, "to know they'll kill you just as sure as that bullet in the brain, only slower. . . . I'm telling you they're evil, and they'll destroy you and those around you."[2] He should know—they destroyed him.

Glossary

addiction—Involuntary psychological, physical, or emotional dependence on a substance that is known by the user to be harmful.

clandestine—Something that is hidden or done in secret.

coca—South American shrub that is used to produce cocaine.

crack baby—An infant born physiologically addicted to crack as a result of the mother having used crack while carrying the baby in her womb.

dopamine—A neurotransmitter, or chemical, in the brain that carries messages between brain cells and regulates physical movement, motivation, emotion, and pleasurable feelings.

drug cartel—A combination of groups who control the production and distribution of drugs.

halfway house—A residence for recovering drug users after their release from a rehabilitation facility. They exist to help patients adjust to living on their own again.

human immunodeficiency virus (HIV)—The virus that infects and destroys T cells in the immune system causing acquired immune deficiency syndrome (AIDS).

incarceration—The process of being imprisoned.

intravenous—Into or within a vein.

snort—Method of taking a drug by inhaling it in powdered form through the nostrils.

solvent—Something that other substances can dissolve into.

synapse—Space between two neurons from two brain cells across which messages are communicated by neurotransmitters.

wired—Very excited and irritable because of the desire to use a drug.

Chapter Notes

Chapter 1. Stories of Cocaine and Crack Abuse

1. Darrell Porter, *Snap Me Perfect! The Darrell Porter Story* (Nashville, Tenn.: Thomas Nelson, Inc., 1984), p. xxii.

2. "Crack Babies in Infancy," n.d., <http://www.focalpress.com/companions/0240804155/crack/crack1.htm> (September 19, 2003).

3. "Yasmine Bleeth: My Battle with Drugs," January 23, 2003, <http://tv.yahoo.com/news/st/20030123/104333400008.html> (September 19, 2003).

4. Ibid.

5. Ibid.

6. "Driesell: Bias ACC's Best Ever," June 20, 1986, <http://www.washingtonpost.com/wp-srv/sports/longterm/memories/bias/launch/bias6.htm> (September 19, 2003).

7. Norma Block, "Somewhere Between Goodie-Goodie and Bad Girl," *NCPS Prevention*, n.d., <www.prevention.gc.ca/en/library/publications/prevention/index.asp?a=v&di=JNTROORG0> (February 20, 2004).

8. Anonymous, "Articles Submitted By Visitors to This Site," March 27, 2003, <http://www.crackreality.com/article.htm> (March 23, 2004).

Chapter 2. History of Cocaine and Crack

1. "A Spoonful of Sugar?" n.d., <http://cocaine.org/cokespoon.htm> (September 19, 2003).

2. Stephanie A. Crockett, "Our Families, Neighborhoods and Communities: Up in Smoke," November 25, 2002, <http://www.bet.com/articles/0,,p164gb4182pg8-4870,00.html> (September 19, 2003).

3. "Sober Adults, Sober Lessons," *Marquette General Health System*, n.d., <http://www.mgh.org/wcc/teensite/adults/articles/fallwin2002/beginnings/sober.html> (February 25, 2004).

4. "Parental Drug Abuse," *Narconon*, n.d., <http://www.narconon-drug-rehab.com/parental-drug-abuse.htm> (February 25, 2004).

Chapter 3. Effects of Cocaine and Crack

1. Narconon of Northern California, "Client Testimonials," *CocaineAbuse.net*, 2002, <http://www.http://www.cocaineabuse.net/client_success.html> (March 23, 2004).

Chapter 4. Producing and Selling Cocaine and Crack

1. Peter Eisner, "Cocaine Trafficker Pablo Escobar Killed in Colombia," December 3, 1993, <http://www-tech.mit.edu/V113/N62/escobar.62w.html> (September 19, 2003).

Chapter 5. Avoiding Drugs and Getting Help

1. Cocaine Anonymous World Services, n.d., <http://www.ca.org> (September 19, 2003).

2. Darrell Porter, *Snap Me Perfect! The Darrell Porter Story* (Nashville, Tenn.: Thomas Nelson, Inc., 1984), p. 259.

Further Reading

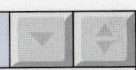

Apel, Melanie Ann. *Cocaine and Your Nose: The Incredibly Disgusting Story.* New York: Rosen Central, 2000.

Barter, James E. *Cocaine and Crack.* Farmington Hills, Mich.: Gale Group, 2001.

Bayer, Linda. *Crack & Cocaine.* Philadelphia: Chelsea House Publishers, 2000.

Connolly, Sean. *Cocaine.* Chicago: Heinemann Library, 2001.

Hyde, Margaret O. and John F. Setaro. *Drugs 101: An Overview For Teens.* Brookfield, Conn.: Milbrook Press, Inc., 2003.

Kerrigan, Michael. *The War Against Drugs.* Broomall, Pa.: Mason Crest Publishers, 2002.

Landau, Elaine. *Cocaine.* New York: Franklin Watts, 2003.

McFarland, Rhoda. *Cocaine.* New York: Rosen Publishing Group, 2000.

Robbins, Paul R. *Crack and Cocaine Drug Dangers.* Berkeley Heights, N.J.: Enslow Publishers, Inc., 2000.

Taylor, Clark and Jan T. Dicks. *House That Crack Built.* San Francisco: Chronicle Books LLC, 1992.

Wagner, Heather Lehr. *Cocaine.* Philadelphia: Chelsea House Publishers, 2003.

Phone Numbers

Cocaine Anonymous
  1–800–347–8998

NAADAC, The Association for Addiction Professionals
  1–800–548–0497

Drug & Alcohol Treatment Referral National Hotline
  1–800–662–4357

National Helplines
  1–800–HELP–111

Narcotics Anonymous
  1–818–773–9999

Index

A
addiction, 10, 12, 15, 19, 22, 27, 29, 34, 36–41
Atlantic Coast Conference, 13

B
Baywatch, 12
Bias, Len, 13–14
Bleeth, Yasmine, 12–13
Bolivia, 32
Boston Celtics, 13
brain, 24–25

C
CBS News, 21
Coca-Cola Company, The, 16
Cocaine Anonymous, 38
coca plant, 16–17, 19, 30–32
Colombia, 30–33
crack babies, 12, 19
crackheads, 19
crack houses, 19
crime, 10, 12, 15, 19, 21, 28–30

D
de Greiff, Gustavo, 31
Driesell, Lefty, 13

E
effects, 12, 24–27, 29, 37, 41
Escobar, Pablo, 31

F
Fellowship of Christian Athletes, 10
forms, 23–24
Freud, Sigmund, 16

G
gangs, 33–34

H
Harrison Narcotics Act, 16
history, 16–22

J
Jordan, Michael, 13

M
markets, 18–19
medical emergencies, 22
Mexico, 33
Moss, Delrish, 19

N
NAADAC, 38
New York Times, 21

P
Peru, 19, 30–32
Pope Leo XIII, 16
Porter, Darrell, 10–11, 43
prevention, 41
price, 18–19, 34
prostitution, 19

R
reasons, 36–37

S
Saint Louis Cardinals, 10
San Francisco General Hospital, 12
Shatz, Nancy, 12
street names, 10, 31

T
trafficking, 30–34, 42
trafficking routes, 18, 32
treatment, 15, 22, 29, 38–41

U
University of Maryland, 13
use, 14, 36, 41–42

V
Vin Mariani, 16

W
warning signs, 37
withdrawal, 15, 19, 39

HOMESTEAD H.S. MEDIA CENTER
4310 HOMESTEAD ROAD
FORT WAYNE, IN 46814